GROLIER
B O O K S

The animals of the Pride Lands gathered once again to pay their respects to the Lion King and his queen. A cub had been born to Simba and Nala.

Rafiki, the wise baboon, raised the cub toward the sun as its parents watched proudly.

The new cub was a lioness—
Princess Kiara was her name. Rafiki
painted Kiara's picture next to that
of her father, Simba. "The circle of
life is complete," Rafiki said.

But was it?

For beyond the Pride Lands lived the Outsiders. They had been banished by Simba for siding with the evil Scar. Zira, a mean-spirited lioness, was their leader. Scar had chosen Zira's cub, Kovu, to be king.

There was news from the Pride Lands—Simba's cub was a girl!

"Perfect!" Zira exclaimed. "Girls will be girls, but boys will be—kings!" Zira planned to reclaim the Pride Lands for the Outsiders, with Kovu as the next lion king.

The months passed quickly, and Kiara grew into an adventurous young lioness eager to explore the Pride Lands.

"Stay in sight of Pride Rock," Simba reminded her as she was about to bound off excitedly.

Simba sent Timon and Pumbaa to watch over her, just in case. But she managed to slip away from her babysitters when they stopped to snack on some grubs.

Suddenly Kiara came face to
face with Kovu! She circled him.
"My father says to never turn your
back on an Outsider."

"Do you always do what daddy
says?" Kovu asked.

Just then, what the cubs thought was a fallen log
moved. It was a crocodile on the attack! Kiara and
Kovu scrambled out of the crocodile's reach.

"We make a good team," Kiara said.

The two cubs began a game of tag.

Just as Kovu was about to tag Kiara, there was a deafening roar. It was Simba! He jumped between the cubs and approached the Outsider.

Then there was another roar. This time it was Zira. The lions faced off.

"I banished you from the Pride Lands," Simba reminded
er. "Take your son and get out."

As Zira turned away, Kovu and Kiara said good-bye to
ach other and sadly returned to their homes.

Back home, Simba scolded his daughter. "You need to be careful," Simba told her. "As future queen—"

"What if I don't want to be queen?" Kiara interrupted.

"That's like saying you don't want to be a lion," Simba replied. "It's in your blood, as I am. We are one."

Becoming queen was a big responsibility, but Kiara wished she and Kovu could have become friends.

Far from Pride Rock, Zira scolded Kovu for being with a Pride Lander.

"I'm sorry," Kovu said. "I thought we could be friends!"

"What an idea!" Zira forgot her anger. Friendship with Kiara was the perfect way to trick Simba into welcoming Kovu into his pride. Then Kovu would replace Simba as king.

The years passed. Under Zira's guidance, Kovu grew into a fierce lion with only one purpose: to reclaim the Pride Lands.

Under Simba's guidance, Kiara also grew up. Today Simba was sending her on her first hunt.

Meanwhile, Zira was watching a fire her lions had set in the distance.

"The plan is in motion," she said to Kovu. "Go!"

Kovu sped off in the direction of the fire. Before long, he found Kiara, who was overcome by the smoke.

Kovu quickly placed her on his back and carried her to safety, where he was met by Simba.

Kovu stepped forward. "I wish to join your pride," he said to the Lion King.

"No! You are an Outsider," was Simba's reply. But the others reminded him that Kovu had saved Kiara's life.

Reluctantly, the Lion King agreed.

It was night when everyone got back to Pride Rock.

"Thanks for saving me today," Kiara said.

"What kind of hunter are you, Princess?"
Kovu asked. "You almost got yourself killed!"

"And I suppose you could teach me?" she
challenged. "All right. We'll start my first lesson
at dawn."

Zira's spies watched Kovu and Kiara begin to form a friendship. They would report that Zira's plan was working.

As the sun rose, Kovu took Kiara out into the
Pride Lands, where the lesson turned into a day of
play. Kovu had never had so much fun in his life!
That night, the friends watched the stars together.

"My father says all the great kings are up there," Kiara told Kovu.

"Do you think Scar is up there?"

"I don't know. My father says there was a darkness in Scar, one he couldn't escape."

Kovu stared at the sky. He wondered if there was a darkness in him, too, as there had been in Scar.

Simba watched Kiara and Kovu from Pride Rock. He was still unsure about the Outsider and worried about the future of his pride. He, too, looked to the stars—and to his father—for guidance.

Nala approached him. "Simba, you want so much to walk the path expected of you," she said. "Remember—Kovu does not."

Nala was right. Kovu was questioning the path Zira had planned for him. Was it evil to follow Zira's teachings—to be like Scar?

Suddenly an arm popped out from a bush. It was Rafiki. "Follow me," he said.

Kiara and Kovu followed him to a beautiful waterfall. There the wise baboon taught the young lions about "Upendi," a special place in the heart that Kiara and Kovu now shared.

Early the next morning, Simba approached Kovu for a lion-to-lion talk.

"Scar couldn't let go of his hate," Simba told the young lion. "But sometimes what's left behind can grow better than the generation before."

Kovu understood: Simba was giving him a chance to prove himself.

That evening, as Simba and Kovu were returning to Pride Rock, Zira emerged.

"Well done, Kovu," Zira scoffed. "You've separated Simba from the others, just as we planned."

"No!" Kovu protested. "I had nothing to do with this!"

Zira's lions attacked. Simba tried to fight them
off, but he was outnumbered. Zira's lieutenant,
Nuka, pursued the Lion King as he scrambled over
a pile of logs.

Simba escaped, hurt but alive.
Nuka was not so lucky.

After the battle, Simba banished
Kovu from the Pride Lands.
"Kovu didn't do it!" Kiara
pleaded. But her father wasn't
willing to listen.

Kiara ran after Kovu and found him by a pool of water. They sat together and watched their reflections. As their images merged, they began to fall in love.

"We are one," Kovu said.

Kiara agreed. "Our place is with our prides. We will unite them again."

Kiara and Kovu
found their two prides
facing off.

"This has to stop!"
Kiara said to the lions.
"We are all part of the
circle of life. We are one."

An Outsider
stepped forward.
"Kiara is right,"
she said to Zira.
Slowly, the other
Outsiders joined
the Pride Landers.

Only Zira refused the offer of peace. She
lunged viciously at Kiara, but missed her target
and tumbled over a ridge.

Kiara reached down to her, but Zira couldn't
reach her paw. The evil lioness fell into the
ravine and was never seen again.

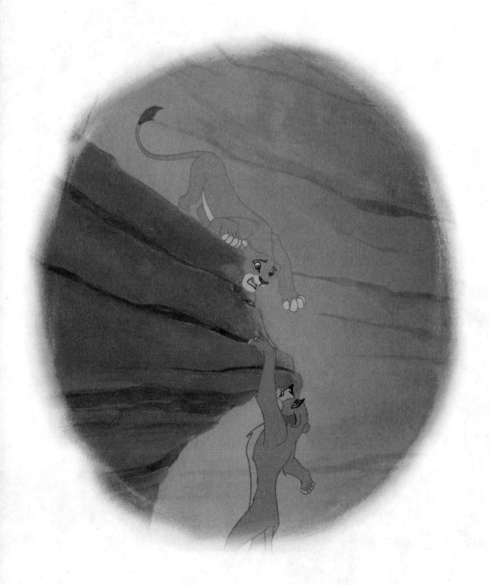

Soon Kiara and Kovu were sitting proudly at the side of Simba and Nala as Rafiki blessed their union.

All the lions looked on with pleasure. Simba's pride had finally been reunited.